A Harlin Quist Book

HERE'S LOOKING AT YOU!

Verses by
Ed Leander

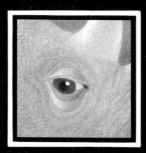

Published by Harlin Quist, Inc.
Distributed by Dial | Delacorte Sales
1 Dag Hammarskjold Plaza, New York 10017
Text and illustrations copyright © 1973
by Harlin Quist | All rights reserved
Library of Congress Catalog Card: 73–80925
SBN Paperback: 8252–0131–4
SBN Library: 8252–0132–0
Color separations
by Vontobel Druck AG, Switzerland
Printed in Holland by Drukkerij Reclame B.V.
Based on an idea by Patrick Couratin

All day long, you look at things:
Animals – people – creatures with wings.
Sometimes they please you, sometimes they scare . . .
But did you ever think? Did you ever dare
To imagine the other point of view?
How you look to the looker who's looking at you?
Some creatures see you as funny and tall.
Some see a section, and that's about all.
So just for the fun of it, glance through this book
And see how peculiar you frequently look.
And while you're about it, try to be bright
And determine which creature is seeing which sight!

1

*Methinks I see some monkey business
Going on out there!
Whatever it is you've got in your hands
I want a bigger share.
I'm hungry – I'm famished – I'm starving
I'm really in terrible shape.
Besides when I see nuts –
Especially peanuts –
I go absolutely ape!*

2

Funny, funny, person!
Don't you know how to talk?
If you can't find the proper words,
Don't worry, I won't squawk.
But right now I'm too busy
To help you practice words.
'Cause Polly wants a cracker –
And you are for the birds!

3

Hello there, you, fluttering by!
Are you trying to catch a cloud in the sky?
Are you trying to reach the silvery moon
And play that it's your own private balloon?
You'll make it, you know,
If some magic day brings
Your own lovely set of colorful wings.

4

Honey, you're a sweet young thing.
Your looks set me a buzzin'.
But why is your face all over the place
So I see you by the dozen?

5

Who goes there, staring into my house?
Who goes there, daring to invade?
You'd better go way
'Cause despite what they say
I'm not in the least bit afraid.

6

Aha! Aho! I'd say hello
But I'm watching you quiver and quake.
Like the fly, you're caught in a web of fear –
Otherwise, why would you shake?
Me, I'm as peaceful as peaceful can be,
Sitting here quietly spinning.
Maybe we'll meet again some other day
And get off to a better beginning.

7

You light me up . . . It's staggering
The lengths to which I'd go for you.
You make me glimmer, flicker, flit –
To tell the truth, I glow for you!

8

Pail and shovel, shovel and pail,
Little one moving so funny and frail.
I'm getting cranky, crabby and dizzy
Watching you look so frantic and frizzy!

9

Hey, you up there on the ceiling,
That must be a very weird feeling
To be turned all around
Looking down on the ground . . .
Does it leave you rocking and reeling?

10

Behave yourself, you terrible person!
Do you want to start me croakin' and cursin'?
Better watch out what you do to me since
I may – you know – turn into a prince!

11

From St. Louis to far-off Siberia,
You scientists hunt for bacteria.
Well, I'd like to mention
Your silly invention
To many of us is inferia!

12

You, there, what big teeth you have!
You make me want to growl.
And as for all the rest of you
Be gone – before I howl!

13

Could you live in rivers? Could you live in seas?
Would you choke on water if you had to sneeze?
Mouth always sucking for food and for air . . .
Something real fishy about this affair!

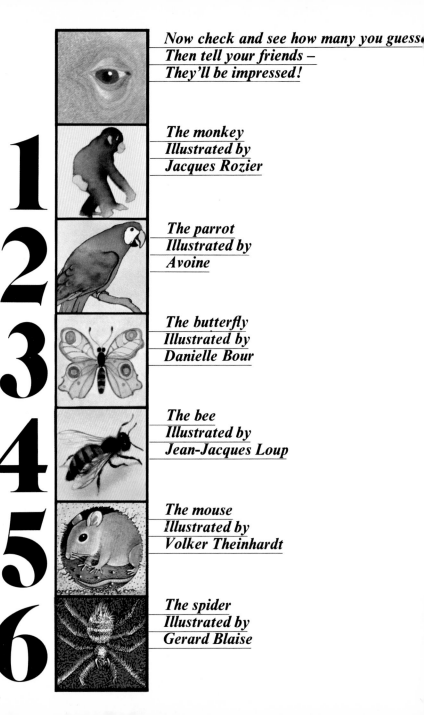

Now check and see how many you guess
Then tell your friends –
They'll be impressed!

1

The monkey
Illustrated by
Jacques Rozier

2

The parrot
Illustrated by
Avoine

3

The butterfly
Illustrated by
Danielle Bour

4

The bee
Illustrated by
Jean-Jacques Loup

5

The mouse
Illustrated by
Volker Theinhardt

6

The spider
Illustrated by
Gerard Blaise

7

8

9

10

11

12

13

The glowworm
Illustrated by
Carlo and Mireille Wieland

The crab
Illustrated by Jean Seisser
and France de Ranchin

The fly
Illustrated by
Louis Bour

The frog
Illustrated by
Michel Quarez

The microbe
Illustrated by
Yvette Pitaud

The wolf
Illustrated by
Claude Lapointe

The fish
Illustrated by
Monique Gaudriault

*Cover illustration
by Henri Galeron
Book designed
by Patrick Couratin*